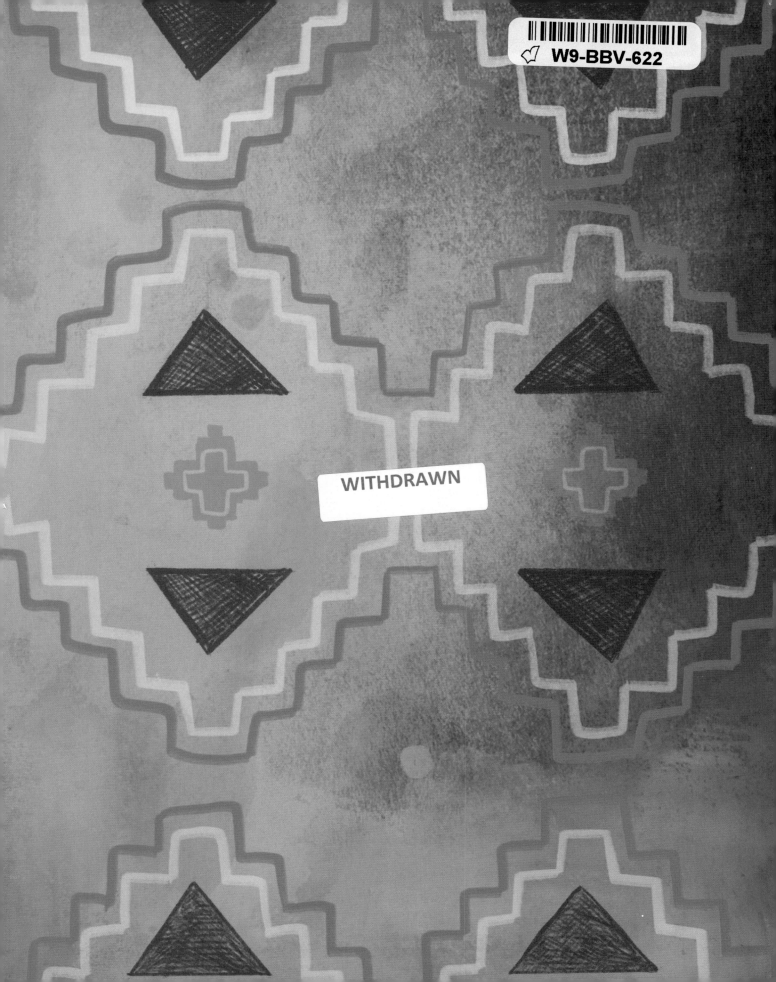

CUENTO
DE LUZ

To my son Luis Miguel, so that he never stops chasing his dreams.
—Lola Walder

To my little star, Yuri.
—Martina Peluso

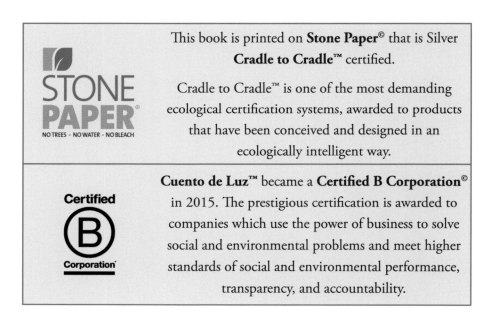

This book is printed on **Stone Paper**© that is Silver **Cradle to Cradle**™ certified.

Cradle to Cradle™ is one of the most demanding ecological certification systems, awarded to products that have been conceived and designed in an ecologically intelligent way.

Cuento de Luz™ became a **Certified B Corporation**© in 2015. The prestigious certification is awarded to companies which use the power of business to solve social and environmental problems and meet higher standards of social and environmental performance, transparency, and accountability.

Juanita - The Girl Who Counted the Stars
Text © 2021 Lola Walder
Illustrations © 2021 Martina Peluso
© 2021 Cuento de Luz SL
Calle Claveles, 10 | Urb. Monteclaro | Pozuelo de Alarcón | 28223 | Madrid | Spain
www.cuentodeluz.com
Original title in Spanish: *Juanita - La niña que contaba estrellas*
English translation by Jon Brokenbrow
ISBN: 978-84-18302-05-3
1st prinitng
Printed in PRC by Shanghai Cheng Printing Company, January 2021, print number 1826-3

JUANITA
THE GIRL WHO COUNTED THE STARS

Lola Walder   Martina Peluso

Juanita lived in Santa Catarina Palopó, a pretty little village next to a beautiful lake, surrounded by three huge volcanoes.

Volcanoes are like massive chimneys made of rock, and when they get angry, they blow lots of fire and smoke up through an enormous hole.

Lake Atitlán is very, very big. At sunset, it shines like the belly of a whale that is sunbathing.

The women of Santa Catarina Palopó helped their families by weaving *huipiles* from silk, wool, and cotton thread. They sold them to the tourists who visited the lake.

Juanita helped her family by cooking. Her mother had taught her how to make delicious, crunchy *tortillas* made with maize that her father brought from the harvest.

In Juanita's village there are no motorbikes or cars. People walk everywhere, and that's why the sky looks so clear, and you can see so many stars at night.

Juanita loved counting the stars. Every night when she finished her dinner, she would run onto the roof of her house, stretch out on an old mattress, and . . . one, two, three, four . . . ten . . . twenty . . . she would count and count, until she heard her mother's voice calling her down.

"Juanita, it's time for bed! You have to get up early tomorrow to go to school!"

But one day, Juanita's mom became very ill, and she couldn't work at her loom. Juanita tried to help her by stitching the *huipil* she had to deliver for Doña Gladys's wedding. But Juanita didn't know how to sew very well and she pricked all her fingers, ending up in floods of tears.

Juanita felt very sad, and climbed up onto the roof to look at the stars. They were so bright, it was as if someone had scrubbed the sky with soap and water. She started to count them: one, two, three . . . but she was so tired, her eyes began to close. Six, seven, eight. She kept counting . . . ten, eleven, twelve . . . until she finally fell asleep.

Suddenly, she heard a bright, glittering voice in her ear. It said: "Juanita, why are you crying?"

Juanita opened her eyes, and was amazed to see a little star right in front of her, looking into her eyes.

"Juanita, why are you crying?" it asked.

"My mom got sick, and the maize harvest was ruined by the rain," said Juanita in a quiet voice, looking at the little star in amazement.

"Tomorrow is Doña Gladys's wedding, and my mother hasn't been able to finish her *huipil*."

The little star looked at Juanita's fingertips, which were full of pinpricks.

"I see. And you don't know how to sew."

"No, I don't," said Juanita sadly, and hid her hands inside the sleeves of her blouse.

"Well, I think I can help you!" said the little star with a big smile.

The little star rubbed two of its points together, until a tiny golden needle fell to the floor.

With this magic needle, Juanita was able to finish Doña Gladys's wedding *huipil* in time. With the money she earned, she was able to buy medicine for her mom.

Thanks to the medicine, her mom got better, and was able to keep sewing and selling *huipiles*. With the money from the *huipiles*, Juanita's dad was able to plant another maize crop. The following year, the maize grew and grew. Juanita was able to cook many *tortillas* in different colors.

Today, Juanita still counts the stars, and although the little star hasn't been back to visit her, every night she winks at a tiny point of light that sparkles in the sky.

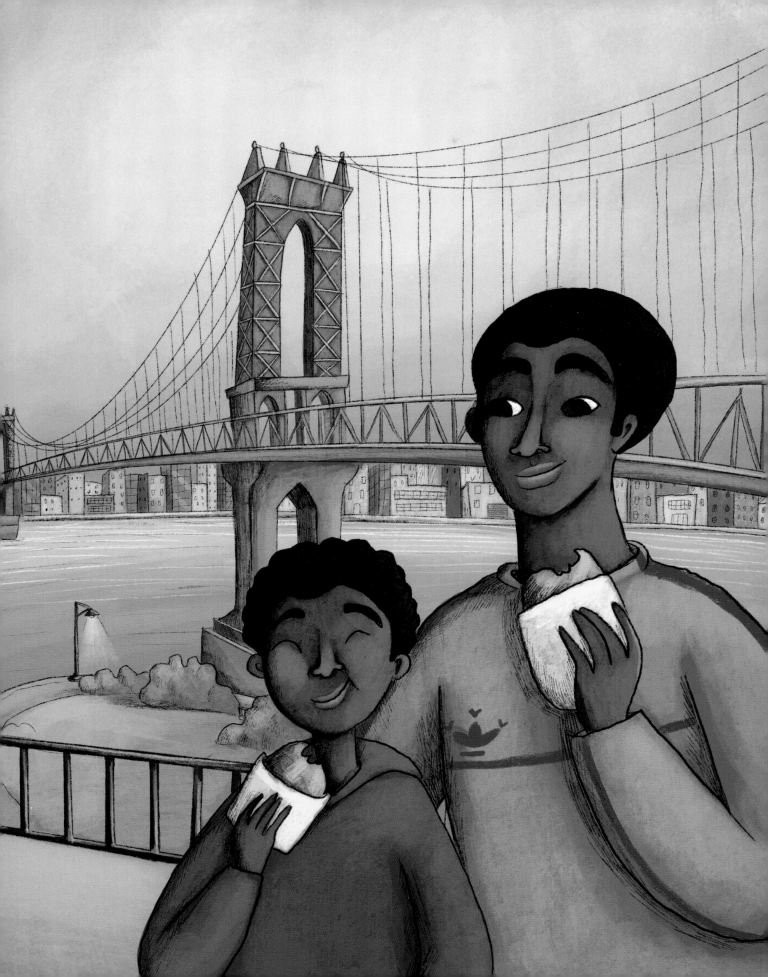

AUTHOR'S NOTE

For a long time, Guatemala has had an important place in my heart. My son has raised a beautiful family there, and I believe that when you love the places you visit, the land gives back that love in the form of unforgettable experiences.

Mayan temples, majestic volcanoes, most of them active, with the heat throbbing inside them, contrast with the lush green of the tropical forests. Rivers and lakes meander through the mountains, ending in breathtaking waterfalls, which naturally sustain the extensive coffee and corn crops.

Corn is the daily bread of Guatemala and the main food for the entire indigenous population throughout the year. Many varieties are grown, and they all are of different colors. The local women make delicious white, yellow, black, and red corn **tortillas**.

The inhabitants of this beautiful country are kind and loving.

I met Juanita one sunny morning. That day, Lake Atitlán woke up slowly, and we quietly sailed away, visiting the small villages that surround the lake. When we arrived in Santa Catarina Palopó, a pretty seven-year-old girl with jet-black hair and a gummy smile—she was missing two of her baby teeth—was sitting on the pier, wearing a beautiful **huipil** embroidered in blue tones. She looked like a little Mayan princess sitting on a wooden throne.

The **huipil** is a square piece of cloth with a hole in the center. Guatemalan women and girls wear it as a blouse, and in each region they weave them in different colors.

Juanita sold woven cotton bracelets. She did it to help her mother, who sat on the floor weaving a few meters away from her, while she rocked to sleep a tiny baby that she was carrying on her back.

Back in Spain, with a head full of memories, the words began to take shape on paper, until Juanita came to form a part of this little tale.

—Lola Walder